SHER
LORD OF THE JUNGLE

SHER

LORD OF THE JUNGLE

EUGÉNIE FENTON

Illustrated by

JOAN KIDDELL - MONROE

ERNEST BENN LIMITED · LONDON

First published 1962
by Ernest Benn Limited
Bouverie House · Fleet Street · London · EC4

© *Eugénie Fenton* 1962

Printed in Great Britain

The story of a tiger who is Lord of the Jungle in the foothills of the Himalaya and how he becomes the godling protector of one of its villages

FOR

RICHARD AND HILARY
AND THE TWO DIANAS

Some Hindu words used in this Book

Baghi *a panther*

Balu *a bear, black with a wide white V on his chest*

Bandar *a small red-brown monkey.* Langur *a larger white and black one*

Barasingh *and* Sambhur *both big stags with wide-spread antlers*

Bhainse *a buffalo, slate-blue in colour, wide horns; bad tempered*

Cheetal *spotted deer.* Chinkara *brown deer.* Kakar *dark-brown deer*

Chi *is the tree-rat or grey squirrel which is also found in England*

Chil *a whistling common kite*

Chua *a rat who lives in the roots of the bamboo*

Gidar *a jackal, slinking tawny in hue.* Lomri *is a fox*

Hathi *an elephant. Male has tusks, but the female none*

Koil *is the Indian cuckoo, a small grey insignificant bird*

Magar *a crocodile to be found in every river*

Mahout *a man who drives and cares for an elephant*

Mahseer *a carp, plentiful in most rivers. Some will weigh over 60 lbs*

Mor *a peacock, often considered sacred on account of its blue plumage*

Murgha *the jungle cock with very brilliant plumage*

Nalah *a dried-up river bed with boulders and a pool or two*

Nilghai *or* blue cow *an ugly blue-black beast with small horns*

Pug *the traces made by a tiger's or leopard's paws*

Sher *a male tiger.* Sherni *a tigress*

SOME HINDU WORDS USED IN THIS BOOK

Suar *the ugly greyish boar of the jungle*
Sal *a tree prized for its wood*
Drongoes, babblers, rollers *all small birds*
Nal *a type of giant couch grass very common*
Siraki *white plumed pampas grass*

Contents

Chapter *I*

A CUB CALLED SHER

THE TIGRESS came to the mouth of the cave and stood there blinking, whilst she accustomed her eyes to the sudden glare after the darkness within. Only a few minutes before, everything had been grey, indefinite, colourless, formless. Then, from over a distant spur, the sun had burst upon the world, had erupted in a fury of dazzling brightness and heat. For a few seconds, the greyness had changed to opalescent green, pink, and yellow. Now the sky was a pale blue.

When the greyness had evaporated, the scenery had become fairyland. From every tree and bush and stunted growth had hung cobwebs; over everything they had been spread like a delicate lace coverlet, and on them, dew had crystallized, shining like diamonds in the dawn. Then, like manna, they were gone. The trees and rocks and grass showed up stark and gaunt and dusty. Another Indian day had begun.

The tigress yawned. She was young and it was her first litter. She was terribly bored with the silly, blind, little things. She opened her mouth and showed her pink gums, her pink up-curving tongue and her beautiful white teeth. Awrrgh! she yawned.

The scenery was lost upon her. All that she knew was that it was a perfect hunting morning. Though, like all cats, her sense of smell was bad, she could scent deer: fat, luscious chinkara. They would be about half a mile away, feeding on the grass at the edge of the jungle. She snuffed again. A sounder of pig had passed by quite recently. She could hear them rootling noisily in the rushes, grunting and squealing. She would have given even one of her whiskers for the runtiest of a codger, for she was very hungry.

A troop of monkeys came into view, swinging from bough to bough and scrambling over the rocks. She had heard them before she had seen them, for Langur, a big monkey with long grey fur and black points, is a chatterer who likes to warn the whole jungle of his presence. He claimed friendship to men. He and his brothers often sat in solemn council, making new laws for the jungle. Everyone else laughed at them, which made the langurs very angry. They chitter-chattered whilst they bounced up and down on a bough, and then they would forget what they had been saying. Each would scratch himself or a friend, searching carefully at the root of every hair in the hope of finding a speck of salt; then off the lot of them would troop whooping and yelling.

Some weeks before, the tigress had snarled at a langur, but before the echo of that snarl had come back, she had been pelted with broken sticks and bits of bark. No self-respecting tigress could stand for that sort of treatment. She had stalked away in a dignified manner, every now and then looking back over her shoulder to snarl at Langur what she thought of him. He and the others followed overhead screaming gutter abuse, till one of them caught sight of Balu rocking and moaning to himself, having over-eaten ripe melon. It was always fun to rag a bear whose sight is poor. He would grunt and growl, throw out his huge arms to try and hug his tormentors, for Langur sometimes came near enough to pull the hair on Balu's back or even his ears. The bear would spin round, pawing and grasping but thin air, whilst the bullies retreated to a safe distance to mock him.

From afar came the scent of a wood fire, that of a woodcutter. Again came the scent of deer, scent of game waiting to be pounced upon; of tender young gazelle, of lordly stag. She was torn between hunger, the desire to hunt, the excitement of the chase, and her mother-instinct. She was full of mother-pride, of jealous possession. She would allow no-one to touch or even come near her precious darlings. It was a curious, upsetting feeling suddenly to have such care and responsibility thrust upon her. Only a few weeks ago she had been a skittish young thing, playing kittenish tricks with her mate, rolling in the long grass, pretending to bite him, and then bounding away, looking back at him over her shoulder prrt-prrting.

She padded backwards and forwards, her tail twitching. She went in to nose her infants, to reassure herself that they were all right. Then out again into the sunshine, to sniff and gaze and tremble with longing. Her paws itched. She couldn't keep still.

The cave had been scoured out of the rock by a river, which long ago had either dried up or diverted its course. The dried-up bed stretched across to a bluff forming a wide nalah full of rocks and boulders and stunted growth. Across this, she could hear the undergrowth rustling as something heavy forced its way through it. A tiger's head and shoulders emerged from the bushes. Immediately all the bristles on the tigress's back went up, her ears lay back flat against her head, her eyes blazed with fury, her tail twitched angrily. She snarled at him not to come any nearer. She was prepared to defend her babies even from him, her mate, for instinct told her that tigers sometimes devoured their young.

He growled back, dragged the carcase of a buck free of the bushes, picked it up by the middle of the back and bounded lightly across the nalah.

At the sight of food, the tigress's snarls changed to purrs. She snatched the buck from him and spat. The tiger smiled, gave a low growl and lumbered off. He had eaten and wanted to drink and sleep.

She dragged the kill into the cave, to where her cubs lay in a hollow scooped out of the sandy floor. Purring with pleasure, she crouched down to eat slowly, daintily. Having eaten her fill, she pulled the skin back over the exposed flesh to keep it safe from flies, and made her way down to a near-by pool.

She crouched down to lap, sipping the water so daintily that she didn't disturb the fish. Every now and then, she lifted her great dripping head and gazed about. She sensed no danger. Everything was quiet except for the twittering of birds. She stood up hesitating, then she walked into deeper water, lay down in it, splashed about, rolling from side to side. A tiger loves a bathe and is a strong swimmer. When she had had enough, she stood up, shook herself and then every paw separately, with sharp little jerks. She settled down to her toilette, licking each paw carefully, cleaning every inch of her beautiful striped coat. She paid special attention to the hollows between the pads and behind her ears. What a difference a good wash made. It was so pleasant to feel clean again, to be rid of all the dust and dirt.

She returned to the cave and lay down beside her cubs, who, sensing her, woke up whimpering, blindly moving their heads, searching for comfort and food. They pushed against each other, barged and toppled over. Then, having found what they wanted lay there with their paws pushing rhythmically against her, their tiny tails twitching. They sucked greedily and visibly increased in roundness. Soon all three lay relaxed, asleep.

When their eyes were open, the cubs became more active. They would stagger about the cave, their baby legs wobbling under the weight of their fat potbellies. They tripped, toppled, rolled over and over. They tagged after their mother, trying to catch the twitching end of her tail. As yet, they were unable to judge distances correctly. With their huge wrinkled paws, they would grab at bats or at a beetle scurrying across the ground. They were beautiful, soft, furry balls, golden dun in colour without any markings.

By the time they were three months old, they romped about,

chased each other, fought savagely with tooth and claw, emitting baby growls ridiculously deep for their size. They would play tag across their mother, and loved to pounce on her ear, which she purposely moved to teach them how to pounce. She would lie there purring, watching them through half closed eyes. When one of them was too rough, she would cuff the offender and send him rolling head over heels. Such a blow from her paw would have felled a man.

The tigerling would pick himself up, shake the sand off his coat, prance about throwing out his legs, and pretend to have an absorbing interest in an imaginary insect. Then, like all young things, he would suddenly tire and fall asleep in a tangle.

When she had occasion to leave the cave, the tigress would miaow to the cubs that on no account were they to stir from it. Off she would go hunting and two bat-eared furries would peep down over the cave ledge at the wonderful world below.

Like all youngsters, they were curious and wanted to find out about things. There was such a lot to look at, to hear, to sniff. They saw the birds who came to peck for seed; the drongoes, the game-cock and Mor the peacock with his bevy of drab-coloured wives. Sometimes they caught a glimpse of Bandar, the brown monkey, and his tribe, swinging from bough to bough, chattering and grunting and whooping. Or Suar and a sounder of young pigs trotting past, tails stiff in the air. Lumri the fox passing by, would pause, lift his sharp pointed head and be off with a whisk of his tail. Gidar, his cousin the jackal, was more impudent. Obsequious, servile, he would yap a compliment which was really a gross insult and slink off, chuckling that he had pulled the whisker of a live tiger.

Shoulder to shoulder the cubs would stand staring in silence, their eyes as big and as round as their ears. Sher, the male, would stretch out a paw to catch Mor's brilliant-hued tail. He

16

swore and spat angrily when he caught nothing. Mor, had seemed to be so near, just within touching distance. Butterflies infuriated him. They invariably fluttered just out of his reach.

One day, the tigress had gone off hunting as usual. Sher saw a blue and orange kingfisher flash past. He sprang at it and toppled over the edge of the ledge. He tried to climb up again, but always fell over on to his back. He stood there forlorn, uttering shrill little miawls.

Feeling adventurous and a wee bit scared, he crept off down one of the paths, halting at every unknown sight or sound. Something moved slowly towards him, staring with horrible glassy eyes, but it never stopped. Puzzled, the tigerling put out a paw and withdrew it in surprise, for the tortoise had vanished into its shell and now looked like a stone.

He came to a shallow pool and saw the reflection of another tigerling. He growled and attacked it and fell in with a tremendous splash. Gulping and sputtering, he struggled to dry land, shaking the water off each paw in turn.

Next he ran his head into a loop of nal, giant couch grass, and couldn't withdraw it. Panicking with terror at being caught, he twisted and threw himself about, pulled and tugged, dug his claws into the earth and almost strangled himself. Gasping he lay still, trying to regain his breath. When he struggled up he found himself free, for he was no longer standing on the other end of the loop.

Soon he had another fright. A rat trying to escape from a snake, dashed past under his nose, and there was the daimon rat snake, its head raised, its tongue a-flicker, its cruel lidless eyes glittering. It rushed past, all seven feet of it, at a terrific speed, slipping over the sand and was gone down a hole. Its foul musty scent tickled Sher's nose and made him sneeze.

He sat down in the middle of the open patch, lifted up his

B

head and miawled piteously for his mother. All round him was but enormous boulders and long grass. Miawl! Miawl! went up his woeful wail. Again and again he howled, till fury changed it to a feeble roar.

A flurry of orange and black leapt out of the jungle, seized him by the scruff of his neck and bounded off with him dangling in mid air, dazed and shaken, unable to move or cry. But at the same time, he felt safe, for he had recognized his mother.

The tigress was in a very bad temper. She had missed her kill and she was very angry with her son. She had heard his piteous cries and had rushed to his rescue, bounding and crashing through the jungle, disturbing all the game.

She shook him as if he was a rat and hurled him to the furthest end of the cave. He felt as if a hurricane had struck him. When he picked himself up and came to snuggle against her, she growled and warned him off.

He sat apart for a while bewildered by all that had happened. He edged his way nearer, an inch at a time, furrowing the sand with his fat tummy. Nearer and nearer he crept, a wary eye on his sleeping mother, till he pushed in beside his sister.

The tigress lifted a paw and laid it across the cubs. A low purring lullaby filled the cave.

For the cubs it was a pleasant life of play in the sunshine, and excitement, for the jungle was full of surprises. Instinct made them watch anything which moved, wait silently quivering, and then pounce upon it.

Sher would wander off by himself, throwing out his paws as he waddled to show his independence. His tubby little body was apt to overbalance. He wobbled, prrt-purring, a Tiger Trot, when suddenly he halted with a gasp.

In the middle of the path stood an enormous monster, glaring

at him with an unwinking, basilisk stare in his vivid scarlet eyes. He was covered with green-brown scales, his stomach a dirty yellowish cream and a black stripe ran down on either side of his spine. Both the latter and his crest stood up in jagged outline. He opened his mouth to show its white inside and his powerful jaws. He chuckled and chortled over the tigerling's terror. It was a dreadful rattle which rumbled all down his throat to the tip of his tail.

For a few minutes Sher, brave like all kittens, stood his ground, his back arched, his lips drawn back spitting. To bolt might be fatal. The monster lifted a huge scaly clawed foot and advanced another step. This was too much for Sher, who bolted into a clump of pampas grass. The iguana went its way.

By personal experience the cubs soon learnt what to avoid, especially insects coloured a vivid scarlet or orange which either stung or tasted unpleasant. They noticed that their mother avoided going near Suar who had sharp tusks, Bhainse the buffalo with his terrible horns, and always the Poison People.

When Sher made his first kill, he was a very proud tigerling. He and his sister had been left to watch whilst their mother drove the deer towards the tiger.

The scattered deer were grazing peacefully when one of them spied the tigress creeping low on her stomach through the grass. The alarm given, the terrified animals leapt and jumped in every direction, panicking as she had intended them to do.

A doe, whose newly born fawn tottering on knobbly, wobbling legs, was still too weak to move fast, pushed and nosed her baby into a hollow hidden deep in the long grass. She nickered to it to keep quite still and silent. Then she went off, leaping deliberately high to draw attention to herself and to lead the enemy away. The fawn, all long, knobbly limbs, lay crumpled looking like knotted, stunted nal.

Sher, as many children do, grew impatient. He was tired of merely watching. He wanted to do something. Imitating his mother, he crept through the grass, uttering little baby growls. He pretended that every shadow and stone was something to be pounced upon. His innocent baby eyes opened wide when the something sprang back and smacked him.

Suddenly he stopped, a fat wrinkled paw lifted. He sniffed and wiggled his nose. There was something very delicious in front of him, something which was alive. Instinct made him gather up his body for a spring. Uttering fierce roars, he sprang. It was a clumsy strike which didn't kill at once. The fawn bleating shrilly, staggered to its feet and tried to run. Sher, his eyes blazing with excitement, watched him. He gave a bound and with his paw made another grab at his prey. The fawn rolled over and lay doggo. So did Sher. He lay there very still, watchful, passing the tip of

21

his pink tongue over his lips. He felt strangely interested in this new plaything, not as yet, realizing that it was food.

The foolish little fawn again scrambled up. Sher gave him another playful tap and began to purr softly. This game went on for a while, till at last, Sher, not yet clever at retracting his claws, hit too hard and drew blood. The fawn collapsed, gasped, gave a shudder and lay still.

Blood . . . Sniff . . . Sniff . . . Blood. The purring changed to growls. The topaz eyes glittered. Their expression changed and their pupils grew enormous. The tigerling's whole being tingled with excitement. He had made his first kill.

Holding the fawn by the neck, he dragged it along between his forelegs as his mother did. Then, he lay down beside it purring with pride, his eyes aglow.

All that day, Sher played with his fawn. He would tap it or roll it backwards and forwards. He was like a soft fluffy kitten playing with a ball; but, when any of the others came near him, his body stiffened, his eyes grew fierce and he snarled a warning.

By the afternoon, his plaything was battered and torn, covered with sand and bits of grass. Sher lost all interest in it.

The little fawn was forgotten by all except the flies, the ants, and the scavenger beetles.

Chapter 2

SHERNI'S SAD END

WHEN THE cubs were nearly full grown, they became restless and would wander off to hunt on their own. The tigress encouraged this independence by refusing to share her kill with them.

One afternoon, they had watched a herd grazing and had singled out their prey, a two-year-old, fat from eating lush winter grass and full of self importance for he had just grown his horns. He grazed a little apart from the others. Several times the leader, an old buck of great experience, warned him of his danger by drumming his hooves and barking. But the young fool knew best.

The tigers hidden in the long grass lay silent, their eyes glittering, only the tips of their tails twitching with excitement. The afternoon sun gilded the glossy coats of the deer, their horns and the tips of their ears. The does moved slowly as they grazed and nibbled, their little ones leaping round them or nuzzling for a drink. Their ears twitched backwards and forwards, their white scuts waggled. Though they appeared to be placid and undisturbed, they were ready to flee at a second's notice. The old buck kept a sharp look-out. His head held high, he sniffed the air whilst he watched for any suspicious movement, for deer live dangerously.

Suddenly he froze and at the same time, all the does, like sprinters toeing the line, dropped their hind-quarters ready to leap away. The buck's nostrils flared, for the wind had veered and he smelt tiger. He gave the signal to scatter by drumming his hoofs on the hard ground. The herd obeyed. With tremendous leaps and bounds, they fled from the danger spot.

Both tigers gave chase. Cleverly, the sherni, the more cunning of the pair, cut out the young buck whilst her brother hunted the others away. Terrified the buck bounded and darted, then tried to double back, leapt high to rejoin his comrades; but always there was the tigress crouching, snarling, ready to pounce upon him.

Frantic with terror he raced on. She liplolloped behind. His heart pounded, his pace grew slower, then his legs began to tire. A kakar is very swift over a short distance, but his swiftness does not last. Sherni knew this. She could hear Sher on her left running parallel. The buck was tiring rapidly. His leaps became lower and lower. He no longer zigzagged. Every time he stopped, she crept up upon him . . . nearer . . . nearer. Coming up on the right, she drove him towards Sher. The hunted beast was unaware of his new danger. His dilated nostrils had lost their sense of smell. He was winded, bewildered. He knew that he was doomed. He stood there trembling.

There was a roar, and with a rush a yellow and black shape hurled itself upon him bearing him down and a massive forepaw twisted his head round breaking his neck. The buck was dead before he knew that he had been struck.

Purr-purring, both settled down to feed. Soon there was nothing left but skin and bone. Two well-fed and contented tigers yawned and stretched. They carefully licked each paw, spreading them out so that the huge claws sprang from between the pads. Both went off down a trail to the river, Sherni leading. Sher stopped to sharpen his claws on a tree. He drew them down, leaving great scores in the bark. It was deeply satisfying.

The track broadened out at a ford. Some flat rocks ran out from the bank into the water. The tigress crouched on one of them, her head and neck sunk low between her shoulders.

It was a lovely peaceful evening. Clumps of tall reeds grew by the bank. The river ran sluggish, smooth and placid in the evening glow, and water lapped over the stone on which Sherni crouched whenever a fish rose and splashed during the evening rise. It rippled behind a swimming snake, and on the sandy beach were the crescent marks of its passing. Its wicked triangular head was held above the water as it swam rapidly across to disappear down a hole. A kingfisher and her three fledglings perched on an overhanging bough. She rose in a flurry of vivid blue and orange, hovered and dived, to rise again with a wriggling bit of silver in her beak. Back to the bough she flew, where the three youngsters with wide open beaks, shrilled for their supper. She showed them how to kill the fish by knocking it sharply against the wood and to eat it head first. One greedy little fellow was too impetuous. He seized the tail and sat there choking, his tiny wings

25

flapped with baby fury whilst his mother dug right down into his crop to remove the obstacle.

As she lapped, Sherni watched some deer drinking on the far bank. They had seen her, but they felt secure with the water between them. Having fed she was merely interested. It was wise to study all game and get to know every animal's character. It was a strange herd. She and Sher had never hunted on the other side of the river. It would be quite easy to cross it, for tigers are very good swimmers.

Two of the young bucks began to quarrel. They grunted and butted each other and made a lot of noise as they splashed in the shallows.

So intent was Sherni watching them, that she was unaware that out of the reeds behind her, a hideous snout followed by a monstrous scaly body had crept silently. It swayed and rocked on its ungainly, short, twisted legs. Only its wicked, cunning little eyes showed that it was alive, not a dead log. It inched towards its prey. Magar knew that he had the tigress cornered if she was not alarmed too soon. Another pace . . . another. The seemingly motionless reptile went into sudden action. He swung about. With a flick of his immensely powerful tail, he swept Sherni from the boulder into the water. Before she could turn to spring back upon land, he was under the water, gripping one of her hind legs in his terrible jaws.

Sherni screamed with rage and pain and terror. She managed to heave herself up on to the rock, but she could not free her leg. She clawed frantically for a hold, for a crack, but the stone had been worn almost smooth by the action of flowing water.

The fighting deer forgot their quarrel. They and the herd bolted for the shelter of the trees. Some fishing cormorants circling overhead came to rest on an overhanging bough like mutes at a funeral. A sandpiper flew up from its nest among the stones

26

squawking with alarm. So did a pair of jays. A kite circled lower to see what all the fuss was about.

Hearing his sister's roars, Sher came bounding. He stopped to watch, blinking. He was uneasy. He didn't know what was the matter. He could see no enemy, and could not understand why she was making such a racket. He sensed that something was wrong. He padded up and down the path, miawling mournfully. Then he stood still, his tail twitching, alert for any sign of attack. Every now and then he lifted up his head and roared.

Sherni went on screaming and howling and clawing at the ungrippable surface. For miles around, her cries were heard, and nervous animals made themselves scarce. She clutched at the wet rock and clung to it with the full weight of her body. If only she could turn round and bite the enemy who held her. A paw lost its grip, slipped, and she felt herself dragged a few more inches further into the water. Magar just held on. His motto was that everything comes to him who waits. It has been the motto of every magar since the first one was hatched, long before Noah launched his ark.

One of the sherni's claws at last found a crack. But her weight tore it off and the pain made her lose her grip for a second. Magar sank a few inches lower. Now only the sherni's head and forequarters were on the stone. She no longer roared. She panted heavily. Soon she became so exhausted that she merely hung on, like tired pullers do on the rope in a tug-of-war.

The sun was setting. Everything was crimson; the ripples of the water; the flat surfaces of the rocks; even the grass appeared to be a-flame. Several animals coming down for their evening drink, paused, puzzled and perplexed. They scented the pacing Sher and fled.

The great struggle went on. Sherni knew that she was doomed. She showed it in the strained look in her eyes. With a last desperate effort, she hurled herself up, frantically clawing at the slippery surface. Her claws broken and bleeding found no grip. She was dragged back into the water thrashing wildly. Magar sank down till his prey was entirely under. He held on firmly in spite of her efforts to free herself. Mud was churned up and through it rose bubbles. When they ceased, the sherni went limp, a very limp, lifeless rag of a tigress.

The sun had set. Everything was quiet and peaceful. A hush came over the jungle. Sher ceased his pacing and padded away.

Chapter 3

JUNGLE LIFE

ONE DAWN when the sky was changing colour and the whole jungle was bathed in a golden haze, Sher silently walked out of the trees into the open grasslands where the buck were grazing. Breathing quickly with excitement, his tail twitching, he picked out his quarry.

Slipping unseen low to the ground between the grass tussocks, he crouched gathering his hind-quarters under him for a spring. The old buck on guard scented him. He flung up his head and snuffed, his nostrils flaring red. He drummed the alarm with his forefeet. The does leapt in all directions. So did Sher. He caught the youngling in his second leap, his great weight bearing him to the ground. The deer's head was twisted and his neck broken before the sun had burst into its flaming glory. This matter of life and death had taken but a few seconds, but the whole jungle was aware that its lord had killed.

The deer barked the alarm, the monkeys whooped, Mor screeched. Every bird and beast gave tongue. It was a babel of howls, grunts, squeaks, twitterings, screeches, barks, and squeals.

Sher dragged his kill to the shadow of some bushes. He lay down to eat, purring loudly as he ripped and tore. By the time he had started on a haunch, the jungle had returned to normal. The deer sensing that he would not kill again, grazed quite unconcerned all around him. Suar and his family went down to the water along the narrow beaten track across which the horns of the kill lay. Sher took not the slightest notice of the piglets as they trotted past in single file. A jungle cock, brilliant in its new plumage, scratched where some grain had been dropped. He called to his hens who arrived in a flurry of excited chucklings and squawkings. Gidar poked his muzzle out from under a bush, sniffed-snuffed and retired.

Sher finished his meal. He dragged what remained of his kill to a tangle of low basonta bushes, scraped a hollow under them and covered what remained of the buck with leaves.

Feeling comfortable and replete, he made his way down to the stream where he drank deeply, had a swim and another drink. He shook himself, licked each mighty paw inch by inch to ensure that they were quite clean. Then he made his way with solemn dignity to his favourite lying-up place in a patch of sweet-scented khush grass. He lay stretched out, his flanks heaving. Occasionally the tip of his tail quivered or a paw jerked as he dreamt.

31

Chua and his brother rats who live in the roots of the bamboos came out to stare. They scampered about chasing each other. One young rat dared to run up onto the sleeper's shoulder and squeaked that he was king of the castle. Sher opened a sleepy eye and closed it again.

A python having newly sloughed its skin, glided and weaved its way in and out of the tussocks and roots. It went slowly for it was purblind and its blunt nose felt sore from knocking against hard stems and stones. Its new skin was very beautiful; also very tender.

A lettuce-green chameleon froze to immobility on a low bough with its long tail coiled up like a spring. It was one with its background. Only its vivid scarlet eyes and the occasional ripple of its white throat showed that it was alive. It was long after the python had passed, that the chameleon lifted a leg in slow motion and put it down a few inches further along the branch, its white paw like the gloved hand of a small child clenched it firmly.

Near-by from the tip of the branch dangled the nest of a weaver-bird. It was beautifully built from grasses and bines. The entrance was at the bottom and it hung from a single strand, a home secure from the attack of any snake. Baya, a cheeky, striated brown and grey rascal, hopped about gaily chirping. He was happy and industrious, quite contented with his humble lot.

A sambhur coming down the trail tossed his head up and halted. He had scented Sher. The whole of his body tensed when he spotted the sleeping feline. With a snort and a kick of his heels he was off, his head back with his antlers lying flat along his neck to avoid catching them in a low branch.

A mongoose poked her sharp nose out of the grass, then her head and her long brindled body. Her sensitive nose twitched and jerked as she smelt the fusty acrid scent left by the python.

She sat up to see better, her head craned forward and twisting. She chattered angrily, her eyes scarlet like those of a cornered rat, her tail fluffed out like a bottle-brush. But no snake answered her challenge. So off she went scuttling and leaping to a ber-tree whose fruit was now ripe.

As the day grew hotter and some of the leaves began to curl the jungle became very quiet for all the animals had retired to the deeper shade to sleep or rest. Bamboos clicked and rattled hollow against each other or exploded when the heat split the old wood. A broad leaf from a sal would flutter down this way and that, rocking on the still air till it finally reached the thick layer of rotting compost. Sometimes a rotten branch broken off by a bird or a monkey came hurtling down, scattering bright petals of orchids, insects, and beetles.

By noon the jungle became absolutely hushed; just a golden-green light filtering through the high branches and the great silence of glades and tall trees. No bird twittered. No animal moved. Yet there was a hidden pulsating life everywhere. Under the rotting leaves, behind the bark, in the mushy wood of fallen trees, insects and beetles hurried and scurried. Some attended to the larvae. The hungry white grubs were always ready for more food. From the branches, from the creepers hung flowers, scented and full of honey; big waxen-white champa, scarlet mowrah and the delicate bronze-violet orchids. Bees and flies buzzed about them greedily feeding and emerged drunk with honey.

Everywhere were butterflies of every hue and shape. They flitted and soared and hovered. A branch was covered with what looked like dead, brown, curled-up leaves. Suddenly the leaves unfolded. A mass of peacock and amber beauty arose and disappeared in the sunlight. On the ground a patch of dead leaves quivered and trembled. A broken flower drifted down upon it,

C

and a cloud of brilliant blue, green, crimson, and canary rose. It swirled like a fairy veil and was gone.

The jungle was so still that one could almost hear the bamboo shoots growing. Each tiny sound was magnified a hundredfold.

Sher was strolling. He was neither hungry nor in a hunting mood. A few weeks previously, the grasslands below the spur had been fired. He wanted to see how tall the young green had grown and what cover he would find when stalking the deer who would go there to graze.

He padded along silently, his great golden eyes missing nothing, not even the praying mantis on a withered stalk of grass. The queer immobile insect with its dry-jointed legs was exactly like the dry-jointed grass it clung to.

He carefully avoided a patch of grass where at the tip of every blade a long thin black thread waved and tried to catch on every animal which touched it. Once a leech gets a hold it will suck the blood of its unfortunate victim.

Sher noticed a quiver in the grass on his left and immediately froze in his tracks when a wicked triangular head rose up showing some six inches of its neck. Its spread hood twisted and turned as it searched for prey. Suddenly the cobra spotted something. Her head darted forward stretched out hovering in the air, her tongue flicker-flickering, sensitive to every scent and stink, her black lidless eyes greedy and glittering.

Sher saw Chi sitting up on a bamboo holding a nut between his forepaws. His back was to the cobra, of whose presence he was blissfully unaware.

Sher saw the hood lower and disappear. The grass undulated in the direction of the squirrel as the snake wriggled her way through it. Again the head rose. She was within striking distance. She lunged forward striking Chi in the back of his neck.

34

The impact flung him to the ground. He rose, shook himself, tottered a few steps and fell, his legs twitching. Then he lay quite still.

Sher shivered. The jungle had suddenly become very cold. He retraced his steps, glancing back to see if the snake was following him. He jerked to a sudden halt hearing a warning hiss. It might be the cobra's mate. But it was only Mynah playing a joke upon him. Mynah was the jungle mimic who loved to tease both man and beast. The little bird flew off cawing with delight, whilst Sher walked gravely on growling to himself.

Chapter 4

SHER MEETS IKKI

IKKI THE porcupine sniffed and snuffed happily to himself as he rootled and poked and nosed about in the thick layer of fallen leaves. Such a lot of tasty titbits could be found in it; huge, fat, juicy grubs, centipedes, beetles and all sorts of larvae, besides succulent roots, fallen petals and fruit.

Ikki's piggy eyes lit up when they spotted a nest of young rats full of little squirming, hairless, pink creatures. Sitting up, he conveyed them with his forepaws one by one to his mouth.

He nibbled and savoured them with appreciation whilst his sensitive nostrils quivered at every scent borne on the light breeze.

There was the smell of fresh, damp earth thrown up by the hoofs of a deer; the strong scent of Suar and his brood who had recently trotted down the trail, the acrid, biting tang of the fresh dropping of a drongo . . . and . . . He sat up stiffly, the tip of his nose wiggling hard. Yes, it was the sweet-sour smell of fresh red meat. Ikki liked fresh meat, and often disputed with Gidar over the remains of a kill.

He cast about circling, his quills lying back flat on his back so that they should not catch in a root or a low-hanging branch. Every now and then, he scratched away among the leaves with his powerful digger forepaws. At last he located it. It was the haunch of a chinkara which Sher had hidden in the bushes.

Ikki dragged his find out onto the path, for he liked plenty of elbow-room, or in his case quill-room when he ate. Nibble. Nibble. Nibble. It was astonishing the rate at which the meat vanished.

Sher came silently down the track for his evening meal. His eyes blazed with fury at the sight of the robber. He growled. Ikki stopped eating, but did not move from where he was. He relied on his quill defences for his safety and knew that all the animals dreaded any contact with him.

Arrgh! warned Sher coming a step nearer.

Ikki chitter-chattered and deliberately turned his back to be in a better position of defence. Sher sprang to attack. Immediately the black and white quills shot up, sharp and cruel. Unable to stop himself, one of Sher's forepaws landed in the middle of them. They pierced his thick skin; one of them ran along the bone up to the elbow joint.

Screaming with pain, Sher drew back and Ikki, lowering his defences, scuttled off into the thick tangle of undergrowth.

38

Savagely Sher tore out all the quills he could. Then, limping on three feet he made his way to one of his lying-up places. He bit and worried and licked his wounded paw, pulling out more bits of quill. One caught by a muscle was dragged further into the wound along with a scrap of dirt from Sher's teeth. His leg began to swell and sharp twinges of pain shot through his shoulder. By the evening all his body throbbed with pain. His paw was swollen to many times its normal size. Any pressure upon it was agony. He had a raging thirst.

He struggled to his feet, but flopped down again snarling and spitting with pain. Already his coat had lost its lustre and sheen. It was dirty and full of dust and dried bits of leaves. The night was one of long, burning agony. However he lay, something pressed on the swelling. His mouth and tongue were dry and blistered. Nasty little eye-flies fluttered and caught in his lashes. A persistent horse-fly settled every now and then on his ear or his flank and nipped.

He could hear the snickering of the grass eaters grazing near at hand, the clicking of their horns, and the whoops of pleasure of Bandar as he leapt from branch to branch. Overhead, high up in the pale-blue sky faded by the hot sun, Chil the kite circled slowly, his wonderful far-seeing eyes missing no detail. Later in the day there was a vulture; then another and another, till the whole scene was filled with the gruesome, hovering, black birds.

Sher's stiff lips snarled back at the sight of them for he knew what their presence portended. But it was a king-crow which made him shake and quake more than any of the others. The solitary little blue-black bird perched near him on a bamboo, his long forked tail with its curved-up ends hanging down. The king-crow was utterly silent. He gazed at the wounded cat with cruel appraising eyes, calculating how long it would be before he died, for he would relish a peck or two for his supper.

39

A small grey bird flew down to perch on a low twig. In a sweet sympathising tone it inquired. 'Did you do it?' repeating his query over and over again till Sher spat at him and he flew away. From the top of a tall sal, a small grey koil shrieked with frenzy a repeated 'Brain fever!' rising in pitch to a delirious E sharp when it stopped from lack of breath to wind itself up again. He had a duet with another koil. 'Anything that you can sing, I can sing higher than you!' The duet soon became a chorus.

Sher had grown so weak that all he could do was to lie and pant. He couldn't even creep into the shade away from the strong blistering sun.

At long last the day was over. It was the hour when a slight breeze soughs through the trees, the hour of 'the raising of the dust by the home-coming cattle', the hour when all in the jungle go down to drink, when all the grass-eaters are on the alert for an attack by Sher or Baghi.

Vaguely, through a mist of pain, Sher was aware of rustlings and slitherings, of the click of horn against a bamboo, the sharp patter of tiny hooves on the hard ground. Birds sang, piped, and flew about pecking, and crowed with triumph when they found a tempting morsel. Soon they would be settling down for the night. An inquisitive cheetal drew back startled when she found herself within feet of Sher's blazing eyes. She leapt away as she had never leapt before.

The jungle grew dark. Others went hunting or grazing. Only Sher lay there, sick and semi-conscious. He didn't even open his eyes when dawn broke.

Chua, the rat who lived among the bamboo roots, came out to stare. Deceived by the tiger's stillness, he took a short cut over the puffed-up leg. The pain of the slight pressure was so intense that it revived Sher. Making a last desperate effort, he bit at his paw savagely. The angry abscess burst and out came the cause of

all the trouble, a jagged piece of quill. Relief was instantaneous. He could feel the poison drain out of his body.

His first thought was of water. He tried to stand up but his legs were too weak to bear his great weight. Creeping, his stomach on the ground, he slowly inched his way down to the stream, stopping and panting, willing himself to make yet another great effort.

He slid down the slope of the bank and landed with a splash in the shallows, alarming the deer who were drinking on the opposite bank. The does started up quivering, each ready to spring away, but the snorting, suspicious buck, his head raised, gave no signal. The stream, too wide for the tiger to clear at one leap, lay between them. By the time he would have swum across it, they could be far away. So they went on drinking.

Sher lay in the cool shallows, too weak at first even to lap. He let the water trickle down his throat to soften the crust formed on his tongue and lips. What a relief it brought to his poor, hot, feverish body! He was content just to lie and let the running water wash out his wound. The hard swelling had gone. Feeling better, he sucked and licked the sore place.

He became aware of the presence of the deer. It annoyed him to see them so near and yet out of his reach. He lifted his great dripping head out of the water and snarl-spat at them. The startled beasts whisked about and were away, all their white scuts a-waggle.

Their fright amused him. He grinned. Slowly he dragged his great body out of the water. He stood up swaying and rocking on his three good legs. A step at a time, his flanks heaving with the exertion, he lurched and staggered to a favourite lying-up place, an open space surrounded by dense bushes in which grew brahmanbuta, a small yellow daisy. It attracted Sher as catmint does a domestic cat. He loved to lie and roll in the foot-high growth, for its crushed leaves gave out a strong, pungent scent. Hindus call it the Flower of God: they apply its juice or a paste of pounded leaves to open wounds, for it is healing and aseptic.

Sher stretched out his paws and thrust them through the cool, soothing leaves. They were crushed and their juice ran over his wound. Relaxing, he was soon fast asleep.

The following morning he felt hungry, very hungry. His paw was still painful and he was too weak to hunt. He knew that if he didn't eat, he would only become weaker. If he could not go after the game, it would have to come to him. So he lay there, pretending to be more sick than he really was, for he had noticed how bold the deer were becoming. One fawn, showing off to its companions had dared to come within a few feet of him.

So, he lay there, spread out like a rag-tiger, his eyes seemingly

closed, but he was able to peer through his lashes. He lay there waiting, watching for an opportunity.

Chi, the striped black and grey tree-rat, skipped down a trunk chitter-chattering, challenging a mongoose to come and catch him. Chi was very proud of his stripes which he had inherited from an ancestor. This reward, so the Hindus said, had been given to the latter by the great god Rama in return for his services in the rescue of his beloved wife, who had been kidnapped by the king of Ceylon. Rama had stroked the great Chi and, wherever his divine fingers had touched him, the hair had grown a glossy black.

Chi hop-skipped and jumped from the tree on to Sher's back. He sat up nibbling a nut. The tiger didn't even twitch for he could see a group of young chinkara watching, their noses and ears quivering with interest. He saw the stupid little deer approach nearer and nearer, their tongues curling round the tufts of lush grass. Nearer they came, Sher felt the breath of one when it blew away a bit of grass which tickled its nose. Motionless he waited, for he wanted to make *quite* sure of his quarry.

One of the chinkara spied a tuft of delicious young growth which almost touched one of the tiger's paws. He hesitated, then sure that his enemy *was* dead, he bent his head down to the grass.

Sher struck, only half raising himself to do so. With his near forepaw, he pinned the chinkara down and bit deep into the neck. The other deer, startled out of their wits, bounded off in all directions.

Chi also fled, chattering shrill with fear and indignation, dropping, as he went, his nut on to the tiger's head.

In spite of his great hunger Sher didn't gobble but fed slowly. He pulled the skin cleanly off the flesh and every bone was stripped of its last scrap of meat by his rasping rough tongue.

Sher, feeling replete, was almost his old self again. He lay there half concealed among the yellow daisies, his great square head resting on his forepaws. He sighed and yawned with contentment. Through his half closed eyes he watched the silly deer who, in spite of their recent fright and tragedy, were again grazing within a few yards of their enemy.

Chapter 5

THE CALL OF SPRING

SHER KILLED twice a week. He grew deeper in chest and colouring. He was now in his prime. If he had been measured he would have been a real viceregal tiger for he was eleven feet from nose tip to tail tip.

Spring came to the jungle. Everywhere the sap was rising and blood ran hot.

Sher was arching his back to get rid of the night's stiffness. He felt lazy and at the same time a curious tingling ran through him. He didn't feel hungry, but there was something lacking.

46

Miaow-w! He growled softly to himself and rolled over on to his back like a foolish cub. Then he sprang up suddenly to sharpen his claws and went off frisking, chasing his own tail. He wished that like a snake he could shed his winter coat. He rolled in the stiff grass to rid himself of any loose hair. Still miawling, he made his way down to a pool for a good swim.

Too engrossed with his personal feelings, he did not notice that all around him in the jungle was mating; that the air was full of bird calls, of whistles and chirrupings, of plaintive notes, amorous trills and the angry sharp strident challenges of young cocks.

In a glade, Mor, all sheen and green-blue-bronze iridescence strutted and paraded, his head with its tiny blue-black crest held high, his thousand-eyed tail spread out in a magnificent wheel behind him. Every now and then he struck the ground with his spurred foot shrilling a p-miawl of self admiration. A covey of dingy-brown hens scurried about, their bodies low, pecking and poking amongst the leaves. They deliberately paid no attention to His Gorgeousness, but each hen had a bright beady eye which missed no glint on his feather, no arrogant strut, no proud attitude. Later, when Mor flew away, his gorgeous tail streaming out behind him, the whole covey meekly followed their lord and master.

In another clearing Murgha the jungle cock was showing off his lovely green, black, and orange tail feathers and the gorgeous sulphur flame and scarlet ones on his breast. The hens huddled in a clacking, clucking group whilst he struck one arrogant pose after another. He drummed with his spurred feet; he flapped his wings; he crowed and made rushes at them. He raised himself on his toes, his vivid scarlet comb swollen and stiff. He crowed a loud challenge to a rival. Another cock, equally gorgeous, equally arrogant, sent a clarion reply and rushed up to combat for the possession of the desirable hens. Each tried to outcrow the other. With heads lowered, feathers fluffed out, they screamed a final challenge and then leapt high in the air in a flurry of attacking beaks and spurs. Up and down, up and down bounced the screeching fighters, slashing at each other with spur and beak. A few feathers fluttered loose. The hen's gossip rose to a shrill cackle. One of the cocks suddenly acknowledged himself to being beaten. He broke off the fight and fled, all long legs and outstretched neck, hotly pursued by his crowing rival till he was out of sight. The instinct of every animal is to follow that which flees from him.

The victor swaggered back chuckling and cock-a-doodling to stamp and parade even more energetically than before, whilst he ogled the hens with a very bright eye. He selected one and rushed at her scattering the others.

Down on Sher's shoulder fell some fiery-red blossoms off a Flame of the Jungle broken off by a pair of fighting babblers. The enraged little thrushes flew at each other, clawing and pecking savagely. They tumbled and somersaulted in a flurry of spread wings and long tails. They shrilled high abuse, pulled out breast feathers and drew blood with their tiny sharp spurs. Lady Babbler, demure in her grey pepper and salt, preened herself on a near-by bough. She ran every feather through her beak, savouring the nits and tiny specks of salt, and all the while she watched the tussle. Now and then she piped a gentle note of encouragement and shook herself so that all her feathers showed themselves to the best advantage. A third cock arrived and slid down on the bough beside her. He chirruped sweet nothings, hopped to her right, hopped to her left and tweaked her on the beak and neck. Suddenly the pair flew off, soaring and circling in an aerial rock-and-roll.

Some way from the babblers, the rollers were enjoying a bathe on the wet grass. The jays, all brilliant blue and orange with touches of black and white, rolled over and over like tumbler pigeons. They soared upwards and came tumbling down in fluffy, coloured balls. They were beautiful to watch, but not to hear, for their shrill, ugly notes grated on a sensitive ear.

Everywhere gorgeous butterflies flitter-fluttered in pairs, hovering, dancing and darting in a graceful minuet up and down the sunbeams. They skimmed and bowed, came together, separated and rose in clouds of dazzling hues, to settle again a little further on with wings folded to conceal their beauty. Only the slightest quivering of their wing-tips and antennae showed that they were not dead leaves.

From a bauhinia, wood pigeon cooed of everlasting love. They

D

bibbled and bubbled and canoodled as they rubbed beak to beak: she modest as any Puritan maid, he in formal grey and slate-blue, his chest puffed out, his scarlet eyes full of pride and jealousy, for a wood-pigeon in love can be as savagely possessive as any other male. There was a note of triumph in his cooing, like the magnificent chords of Mendelssohn's Wedding March.

The deer also heard the call of Spring. In every glade and ride were young bucks trying out the strength of their new horns. They roared and bellowed, struck the ground with their fore-feet and rushed together, lowered forehead against forehead, antlers interlocking. Each pushed, trying to get the better of the other and their white scuts wiggled furiously. The does stood on one side to watch with their beautiful brown eyes, their nostrils wiggled as they caught the cool fresh scents of Spring. How handsome, how magnificent were the males! The cheetal with his white spots on shining cinnamon; the sleek, glossy kakar; the deep-brown, huge antlered sambhur and the slate-blue, almost black nilghai. The does were quite willing to follow whoever the victor would be, for he would be a strong and wise leader.

Even Suar was going a-courting. The boar with his sharp curved tusks, his wicked little piggy eyes, his tail stiffly vertical, trotted round his ugly bride. He poked her in the ribs with his snout; rode her off like a polo pony, grunted and blew and made queer piggy noises to which she replied in sweet porcine tones. Sometimes a young boar would crash out of the undergrowth, eager to woo her, but after one look at her veteran lover would hurriedly retreat.

On a patch of sand in a nalah, a couple of cobras wriggled in a Spring dance. Sher halted to watch them, mesmerised and curious. Their beautiful sinuous bodies were intertwined. They rose and fell and curtsied. Their heads with their hoods out-spread bobbed to and fro, their tongues flickering. They hovered and kissed and swayed to a gentle hissing. Vishnu's spectacles on the back of each hood glittered as if newly painted. Sher could see the scales slip in and out, under and over each other with every sinuous movement. Exercising great strength of will, he turned away his head from the fascinating sight and, with a deep sigh of relief, went off.

He was in a distant valley when he heard a new sound. He halted one paw in the air, wondering what it was. It came again, vibrating through the jungle and he knew that it was the call of a young tigress. Again it sounded. He bounded off in its direction.

As he leapt along, he felt his skin tingle, his blood race hot. His whole being ached with desire. Again and again the soft purring throbbed on the still air, a maddening purring which re-echoed off the low spurs. Now it was to his right . . . to his left . . . in front . . . behind. He turned and twisted and cast about, answering her calls with roars of thunder.

Suddenly he came upon her standing in a glade with the sun shining on her beautiful, glossy coat. He capered up to her to show off his fine points. She prrt-prrted. He miaw-growled. He was about to nuzzle her nose to nose, when there was a crashing through the scrub and another tiger appeared on the scene. He was old, mangy, and scarred. His once fine coat had faded to a dingy dun. The edges of his ears were torn. Some of his teeth were missing.

The two suitors eyed each other, the hair along their chines stiffly erect. They stood sideways to each other, their ears flat back, their tails twitching angrily. They growled low, deep down in their throats. Their flanks heaved, but otherwise they didn't move.

The old tiger was cunning. He had more experience. He knew when and how to strike to the best advantage, but he knew also that his stroke was much slower than it used to be. Sher prided himself on his enormous strength and agility.

They stood there for a long while, snarling and rumbling, waiting to spring. She lay down to watch, her beautiful eyes clear and golden.

Suddenly the old tiger realized that he would come off worse in such a fight. With a growl and a shake of his head he turned and walked slowly, very slowly away.

Sher's angry stiffness changed. The hair flattened on his back as he relaxed. He gave a last warning roar but made no attack. He was the victor.

The little tigress smiled. She purred and came to rub herself against the flank of her beautiful lover. They sniffed and rubbed noses. She gave him a playful pat and leapt nimbly sideways. He followed trying to caress her. They frisked up and down the glade, both growl-purring to show their pleasure.

Hot and panting they stopped to stand a little apart. She minced off sideways, rolled over with one shoulder to the ground, her eyes half closed. Prrt! Prrt! she invited. He strode up to her, his eyes glittering like blazing topazes. As soon as he was within reach she slapped him back with her paw and rolled about in a ball catching her tail. Tiring suddenly of this game, she was up, streaking in and out of the bushes. They had a lover's sparring match of gentle clawing and nibbling of ears and necks. Then they lay down panting and blinking in the sun.

Sher purr-growled. She prrt-prrted, admired her claws, wiggled the muscles of a shoulder and turned her back on him to show that she was not really interested in his proposal. He rose to his feet and stood there, growling. Then he turned and slowly walked some way down the glade. Prrt! Prrt! She called softly. With a show of dignity he returned and lay down to watch her roll on her back and show off the lovely thick creamy fur of

her stomach. He put out a paw and touched it. Immediately she drew up all four paws together and pretended to bite him. She miawled. He growled.

Suddenly they sprang to their feet. Shoulder to shoulder, they trotted off down a trail to her favourite place, a patch of long scented grass in a circle of Pampas grass.

Chapter 6

THE VILLAGE GODLING

LIKE ALL in the jungle, Sher avoided Man. He was the un-
known. Everyone, man or beast, is suspicious and a bit afraid of
what he does not know.

Sher tolerated Man as long as the latter did not interfere with
him. At the same time, like all cats, he was intensely inquisitive
about him, for much of jungle life depends on man's doings. If
the undergrowth was cleared, or new fire-rides cut, or fresh land
put into cultivation, the herds moved away. When the young
green corn showed in the furrows, or the melons and cucumbers

ripened, then the kakar and cheetal grazed near the villages, braving the bull-roarers and yells of the watchmen.

Sher knew by sight all the villagers who lived near his hunting grounds: the woodcutters and the herdsmen, the peasants who went out to plough and work in the fields, the women who weeded and tended the terraces near their homes, and those who collected leaves for cattle fodder.

He often stopped to watch the priest, who lived by a sacred stone under a spreading fig-tree. Greatly intrigued, he would watch the bare-headed Brahmin in his saffron robes wash and anoint the god, lay offerings – flowers, a few grains of rice, some cardamoms – before it and heard the tinkle of his bell, which he rang to summon the god.

Sher was particularly interested in old Budu, the hunter, who spent many hours in the jungle following spoors and who always carried an ancient muzzle-loader. He sensed that he could be dangerous if annoyed. Budu could describe every cheetal and kakar, every tiger, leopard, and bear within a radius of twenty-five miles. He knew their lying-up places, their tracks, their behaviour. He could move as silently as Sher himself.

Sometimes the two would meet in a clearing. Sher would halt and stare; then uneasily he would slowly turn his great square head away, give a disdainful arrgh! and vanish. Budu would stand quite still, with his palms together in salutation to the Lord of the Jungle, and perhaps wonder where the sherni was.

Sher was making his way down through the terraced fields. Sushila, a ten-year-old girl was weeding an onion patch. Her baby brother lay in a corner of the wall on his back, kicking and chortling and sucking his big toe, as all babies do.

Sher, spotting the little naked thing crept up to investigate, for he was curious. He sniffed and pushed the baby over with his nose. He didn't like the smell of the castor-oil which had been rubbed over him. He was quite taken aback by Sushila's shrieks and the flapping of her dopatta (head kerchief) as she tried to beat him off. The courageous little girl had seen the tawny shape slinking along the wall, and had come to the rescue of her brother. The sound of a human voice always terrifies any wild animal. Sher had spat-snarled and fled. Afterwards, he always kept clear of Sushila and her terrible white flapping thing.

One dawn Sher was lying curled round on a path fast asleep. Old Mai-ji, a widow on her way to market, was carrying a laden basket on her head. In it were some ripe heads of maize, peppery white radishes, some homespun skeins of cotton and a tin full of freshly ground red pepper. Rounding a boulder, she almost stepped on the sleeping tiger.

Shrieking. 'Hari Bol! Have mercy, Lord Khrishna!' she fainted. The contents of her basket flew in all directions, and the red powder fell over Sher's face. The surprised, so rudely awakened tiger roared to his feet, sneezing and blinking; he turned and fled, still sneezing to rid himself of the terrible stuff which stung his eyes and made his mouth and nose feel as if a flaming torch had touched them. Roaring and swearing with pain and fury, he plunged into a pool, rolled and splashed in it. Feeling a little better but still sputtering and gasping, he cantered off to his secret lying-up place.

When Mai-ji was found by a couple of villagers, she told a rambling story about a tiger who was Hari Bol, the great Lord Khrishna himself. He had told her that he would protect the village and that they must make him their godling.

The villagers, being both ignorant and superstitious, were only too willing to believe in such a miracle. They were also encouraged by the priest, who hoped to profit by more offerings to his temple. Only Budu was sceptical. He had recognized Sher's pugs and had tracked him both to the pool and to his lair. He knew also that he had killed on the preceding evening, and so had not been hungry.

Shortly after this incident, Sher was lying on a rock overlooking another path. It was a favourite spot of his for it was warm in the early morning. Lazily he watched a couple of men come into view walking one behind the other. They were strangers. One of them had a tiger skin wrapped round him. As he emerged from a patch of dense shade into the strong sunlight, Sher was deceived into thinking that he was another tiger.

With a roar he leaped, felling the man to the ground and his sharp claws slashed the naked body. His companion fled shrieking, a foolish thing to do, for Sher was after him and in a couple of bounds he caught up with him. He pawed the bodies over, then, deciding that he did not like their reek of rancid oil and strong tobacco, went off to hunt.

About an hour later the bodies were found by a herd and near them a sack of silver coins and jewellery. Very little work was done that day for everyone stood about in excited groups gossiping, shouting, and arguing. A week previously a couple of holy men had arrived in the village, men regarded with great favour by the gods. They performed many miracles, all by cunning sleight-of-hand. Then the whisper went round that they could change brass into silver and silver into gold. It was an old trick, the same used by gypsies to dupe silly people.

The method they used was to bury the articles in an earthenware pot under the ashes of their fire. The pot was to be left there for a whole month otherwise its contents would vanish. It was only when a sack full of village property was found near one of Sher's victims that the villagers realized how they had been duped. More than ever now were they convinced that the tiger was indeed their protective godling.

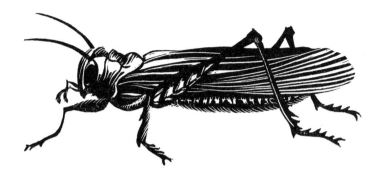

Chapter 7

THE LOCUSTS

THE TWO tigers were lying up in a grassy patch on a spur. It was a favourite spot of theirs during the cold weather, for the grass was soft and the sun not too hot. From it they had a good view of the village and the fields below it.

Sher lifted his head, yawned and watched the sherni uncurl herself, stretch first one shoulder, then the other; roll over and rub her back in a delicious grass bath. She was a sleek and beautiful cat, clever and cunning, with just the right feline temperament to tease, egg on, plague, pester, and delight her royal lord.

It was a lovely afternoon, very quiet up on the spur except for the incessant chirring of crickets, the soft soughing sigh of a ghost of a breeze. Once a hare came hopping high, his long ears a-flop, his legs all angles. Spotting the tigers, he whistled shrilly through his front teeth and was off jinking here, twisting there. He crushed a plant of artemisia, for its pungent aromatic scent billowed and spread.

Suddenly Sher sprang to his feet. The sherni stopped her rolling and watched him with anxious eyes, all her senses alert. Perhaps he had been stung by ants. His ears moved. He sniffed. He gazed about. He sensed something. His whole being reacted to an unknown, unseen danger. He shivered when a shadow swept over the spur and the sun was blotted out; yet the sky was quite clear. He paced to and fro uneasily. Again he stood still, watching. Looking up he saw several curious ragged patches of cloud travelling very fast, yet there was no wind.

Shouts came from where the peasants were working in the fields. He could see men running, waving their arms, heard their shouts of alarm and urgency. Men, women, and children poured out of the village screaming and yelling. They carried sticks. They beat on tin trays, drums, and empty kerosene tins. The din they made was terrific as they rushed out into the fields. Sher could hear the raucous rattle of Bishen's bull-roarer and someone was swinging the great bell from the temple. Clang! Clang! CLANG! Even the priest was there with his conch-shell and the bellow from it out-blasted the blare of everything else.

Something light tickled the tiger's ear, another fell on his back and a third entangled itself in his whiskers. Sher angrily brushed it away with his paw and crouched low to avoid a flurry of insects which alighted on his nose, eyes, and ears. All over him were locusts; the air was thick with them flying. They covered the grass and ground, crawled into everything. They were really rather beautiful with hard, gleaming pea-green bodies and immense, transparent gossamer wings veined with red. Sher wasn't afraid of them. They didn't bite and were easily crushed. But it was their numbers and their persistence that annoyed him. He also became conscious of a new sound, of a curious soft hissing, that of thousands and thousands of tiny jaws munching.

A few minutes ago all around him had been lush long grass. It had vanished. Now only bare earth and stones remained, with the locusts jostling and climbing over each other.

When the villagers had killed or driven away most of the marauders, Sher saw the women and children collect in baskets any which remained to dry in the sun and to be eaten later in curries.

As Sher made his way down to the river for a drink, he saw many a peasant stand and stare at his bare field, a sad sight of stripped stalks. Not a trace of green remained where an hour before there had been a promising crop. Now, there would be no harvest of winter-sown wheat and millet.

If an ill wind had blown the locusts to the fields there were many who rejoiced. All the birds pecked and gorged. They sang and whistled and trilled with joy. Even Murgha had no need to cluck to his wives. He just gobbled and choked and gobbled again as soon as his throat was clear. Suar and his piglets came down to rootle. They guzzled and gulped noisily crunching and eating everything greedily, wings and shells and feet. Now and then a piglet choked when something had gone down the wrong way. He would stand there stiff, his eyes bulging, till he was able to breathe again.

Balu came down to gorge and made a glutton of himself for a fat oily locust was even more tasty than a white grub. Lizards darted here and there to pounce on a fat, crawling locust whose wings had been damaged. One of them stood with a half swallowed insect sticking out of his mouth. He was too gorged to gulp it down. Their tummies were swollen and their eyes bulged from over-eating. Even the chameleons moved swiftly to catch the odd locusts who had wandered deeper in the jungle.

Sher padded off to the grazing grounds. These had been stripped more bare than if all the deer in India had cropped them. There was not a single blade of grass, not a head of grain, not a leaf left on bush or tree. He felt more and more uneasy. Like all animals a tiger is set in his habits. He dislikes having to change his hunting grounds.

For a month the tigers hunted as they had done before the coming of the locusts. Then the game became scarce and many of the village cattle died once the reserves in the byres had been eaten. The villagers became thin and haggard and ill. No one sang. All the small drums were silent.

Then the locusts came again to devour the tiny shoots of green grass just showing above the earth. They were the hatch-out of the eggs laid by those of the first flight which had escaped. They were the hoppers unable to fly as yet. The whole ground was covered with their oily yellow-green bodies crawling over each other, ever advancing, unbeaten, unstoppable. They were like a seething mass of pease pudding in which the villagers waded up to their calves. Wherever there was a tree this yellow foulness climbed it to a height of five feet, falling and slipping back, whilst others filled the gaps. Sher spat and sneezed and growled as he slithered on the oily, greasy bodies.

This time the villagers beat neither drum nor tin. Everyone turned out to dig deep trenches. They filled them with burning wood, and drove or swept the scourge into them. But for a hundred locusts which were burnt, a thousand crossed over their charred bodies. A trench became filled within minutes. Everything reeked of the burning oily flesh, and of the low, whirling billows of smoke from the kerosene-drenched wood.

The fight against the plague went on for several days. Every animal in the jungle was disturbed and fled from the noise and the flames.

62

Chapter 8

FIRE! FIRE!

IT WAS midday, the noon of a hot sweltering June, before the break of the monsoon. It was blistering hot. The winter rains had failed, so all the shallow-rooted growth had dried up and died. Only a trickle seeped down from the waterfall; the pools in the narrow glen had shrunk to almost nothing. Many of the grass-eaters had moved away to where the grazing was more plentiful.

Sher, being a creature of habit, had not changed his hunting-grounds, though every kill was barely worth the effort. He and his mate lay stretched out in the scanty shade of the lantana, the low-growing scrub of the foothills. At dawn, they had killed a miserable kakar, mere skin and bone.

Like all sensible jungle creatures they lay up during the heat of the day. The hard ground hurt their thin, gaunt bodies. The flies were maddening with their buzzing and stinging. A small beetle crept into the sherni's ear, driving her nearly crazy till it fell out. The still hot air was solid and breathless. It was difficult to relax. Both animals panted, their lower jaws fallen, their tongues lolling. Their beautiful coats had lost their gloss.

Suddenly Sher woke and sprang up. There was none of that arching of his back, the leisurely stretching and flexing of his muscles to rid them of their stiffness, none of that contemptuous lazy yawning. Instead, his eyes, ears, and nose were keen, alert; his fierce white whiskers bristled like antennae. Everything about him was tense and strained; the nervous twitching of the tip of his tail showed how uneasy he was. He was aware that some danger threatened. Yet the jungle was still and calm. Nothing stirred in it, except the ants and other insects. He could neither see nor hear anything unusual, but instinct made all the hairs along his spine bristle. He growled low to himself and padded backwards and forwards, his lower jaw sagging.

There was no wind, yet a faint smell of wood-smoke came and went; just the ghostliest of whiffs. It came stronger. Some agitated kakar rushed by, bounding and leaping, quite unconscious of the presence of their greatest enemy. The does butted and pushed on their weary fawns; they licked their flanks to urge them to make greater efforts. A nilghai came barging and stumbling through the low scrub, terror in its eyes and flaring nostrils. It puffed and snorted at the sight of the tigers, tried to back, then plunged off sideways.

A troop of monkeys, strangely silent for once, hurried after an old male whose coat was mangy and scarred. Two of the females carried babies who clung to the long hair of their stomachs. They were piteous little beings, wizened and almost naked but for

E

silky down. An old female sneezed when she saw Sher and whimpered softly to herself. Already, she was feeling the pace. Every time she leapt was a greater effort; once she had nearly missed her footing. The younger monkeys were too scared to stop to pelt their enemy with sticks; each was anxious not to miss his turn on the branch to swing across to the next tree, for like Chi, Bandar has his recognized routes from tree to tree. When one of them hesitated or stopped, the old leader would rush at him barking with his teeth bared. He was a firm disciplinarian and would stand no nonsense or disobedience.

Suar trotted down the path leading his file of young porkers, every tail held at the vertical. Bhainse thundered heavily down a slope and stood at the bottom, her head lowered blowing angrily through her nose and a great fear in her cold blue eyes. On the buffalo crushed until she was out of sight.

Sher stopped his pacing. The danger must be great to have disturbed both Suar and Bhainse. It would be wise to follow their example. As the two tigers moved off in a dignified walk down the game track, the first billow of smoke came over the spur. They could hear the crackle and roar of the flames behind it. A queer red light blotted out the sunshine.

The alarm now became general. All were in flight from the common enemy. Mor and his hens, Murgha and his wives scurried out from under the bushes where they had been roosting. They scuttled along the fire-break with long leggy strides, every now and then taking to their wings for a short distance. Out of every tree and bush flew birds. Butterflies rose in their thousands. The air was full of flittering, fluttering shapes. Every fallen leaf and twig, every bit of rotting wood, every vine and bine came alive with insects, small reptiles and all manner of slow-moving creatures who were sensitive to the higher temperature. Many tried to

66

burrow down deeper, to take refuge under stones or vanished in narrow crevices.

A python slithered off a branch round which he had been coiled. With surprising swiftness he darted for a boulder in the middle of a pool in the valley where he hoped to find safety.

The dignified walk of the tigers changed to a canter, then to the swiftest pace the felines could muster. A tiger can travel enormous distances but he must do so in his own chosen slow lope. His charge can be overwhelming over a short distance, twenty or thirty yards. His muscles have great power but no lasting stamina. Like all felines, Sher liked to look down from a height. So he made for the rocks crowning a high spur from which he could see across a valley and over the next spur which was much lower. He flung himself down, panting heavily from his

67

exertions, his ribs heaving. He looked anxious, afraid of the un-known. The sherni whined and huddled close to her lord.

The first signs of the enemy appeared on the lower spur. The tops of the trees growing on its further side writhed in the air as if a giant was twisting their roots. They collapsed and a shower of sparks belched up. The next moment the whole ridge was on fire. The immense candelabra cacti looked like Jewish minorah lit for the Festival of Lights. There were flames everywhere, greedy, devouring flames which came roaring up the higher spur. The fire was closing in upon them in a pincer movement.

Sher charged across a narrow strip of burning grass to more open country of rock and boulder where there was nothing to catch fire. Miawling with terror the sherni followed. Both animals shook themselves free of sparks and stood panting, uncertain of what to do next. The smoke swirling around them made them cough.

Sher stood still, his ears back, snarling, uneasy. The sherni dashed about, always to be beaten back by a fresh outburst of flame. At last she crept along the ground to him, miawling for comfort.

They watched the flames approach a narrow dip. The smoke billowed upwards as the hot air from below rolled it up. Then the flames crept down via grass and shrub insidiously, unob-served, to flare up suddenly on the nearer slope, to charge up it almost invisible in the strong sunlight. They left behind them a desolation of twisted, charred branches and ashes. The heat was terrific.

The fire gained rapidly sweeping to tree-tops. It leapt across the grass for everything was sere and brittle-dry. Huge spurting flames darted out of the choking red smoke to secure another hold. Bamboos cracked and exploded. There was a sinister

68

whoosh! when the flames rushed up a tree, devouring its curling leaves, or a crash when a big branch fell: sparks and burning wood spattered out through the smoke, spreading more destruction.

The ride was a fantastic sight of terrified animals, leaping and bounding, cantering and scuttling. Sher went in the company of a nilghai and a buffalo calf. He felt something on his back, but was quite unaware that it was a monkey, nor did the latter know that he was riding a tiger. Here and there, flames tried to run across the grass of the ride, but the stampeding animals stamped them out before they could get a hold.

Some of the deer plunged into the further jungle to escape from the smoke and heat, but most just followed the leaders. Many of the birds and dozens of the younger and weaker animals were caught before they could reach the safety of the ride. Their shrill screams went unheard above the roar of the flames.

At the edge of the ride was an immense sal, a lovely tree with huge, flat leaves. As the flames leapt up it one of the flaming branches broke off and landed on the antlers of a barasingh. He jerked up his head at this fresh terror, thereby wedging the branch more securely between his horns. To rid himself of the enemy, he dashed into the further jungle to brush it off against a tree.

The fire was across the ride.

Sher plunged off down a track growl-miawling to his mate to follow. The trail led nowhere. They had to crash through bush and bamboo tearing their coats against the sharp thorns. Only the sheer weight of their bodies carried them through the tangled growth.

Sher, his beautiful coat singed and torn, at long last plunged down the slope to the river alone, for the sherni was lost in the inferno. In normal times the river would have been half a mile in width. Now, it was shrunk to a couple of narrow, deepish streams with a long spit of land between them. On this all who could do so had taken refuge. Men from a near-by village had driven down their flocks and herds to it. All carried their most precious possessions be it but a spinning wheel or a terracotta pot. With much apprehension they viewed the invasion from the jungle. The further stream was too swift to swim across it safely.

Perched on the rump of a buffalo was a little girl of six. Her older sister had just driven a pair of goats down to the shore, when Sher bounded beside them. The child gave the tiger a slap on the rump for him to make more room for her precious goats. She nearly collapsed from fright when he half turned round and spat at her. Her shrill screams terrified him even more than had done the flames.

With a resounding roar he plunged into the water, avoided the spit of land and soon reached the other bank.

Chapter 9

THE MEAL THAT WASN'T

AFTER THE disastrous forest fire, Sher changed his hunting-grounds for a while. He felt lonely and missed the familiar trails and watering places. Also he had to be wary, for a stranger is always looked upon with suspicion.

In the mist of an early dawn, he topped a rise and looked down on to a camp where the jungle had been cleared. It was a sal forest and elephants had been brought in to drag and stack timber.

They were picketed in two long lines in front of the bamboo and reed huts of the mahouts, their drivers. His eyes glittered at the sight of so many elephants who stood swaying and rocking from foot to foot, their grey trunks snaking out for the green stuff piled in front of them. If there is something which a tiger is partial to, it is elephant calf, a rare delicacy extremely difficult to procure, for the wise mothers take great precautions to safeguard their young.

Sher lay there watching the mahouts feed their charges, take them down to the river for a swim and a good scrub all over. For days, he slipped under cover of low brushwood to spy on the elephants at work. He saw the chains fastened to the hewn trees and the elephants drag them down the clearings to where they were stacked ready to be floated down-stream. At a word from his mahout, Hathi the elephant would curb his trunk under the log till he had reached the point of balance. He would lift it and place it on a pile. Later, in the evening, moving as silently as ghosts, the elephants would return to camp carrying great bundles of grass and branches.

Soon the tiger knew all about the bustle and order of camp life; of the small wood fires, the kneading and baking of bannocks, the cooking by the women of stews in huge iron cauldrons. There was much bustle by the tents, where men came and went, talked and shouted. Some of them were strange white men, others jungle folk.

Every evening a mail runner came in panting, the heavy bag slung across his bare shoulder, the spear with its jingle of bells in his hand. Once or twice, Sher had met and passed him with a snarl. He hadn't liked the sound of those bells or the sight of the sharp, shining spear. The runner had reported the presence of a tiger. Orders had been issued to take extra precautions.

Many of the mahouts slept by their charges. When an elephant grew restless, the mahout would speak to him, call him the son of an owl, tighten up the fragile hobble, a twist of jungle grass, and lie down again rolled up in a blanket from head to toes.

Sher soon spotted a mother-to-be. She stood at the end of the line with another female who would act as auntie. The mahout in charge of her brought her all sorts of titbits: young bamboo shoots, handfuls of sugar or bread. He told her that she was his Pearl amongst elephants, how fine her son would be, and how, one day, he would carry the golden howdah of a great maharajah. She stood there rocking, her ears flapping slowly, her small eyes betraying anxiety.

Sher could see her massive grey shape loom up in the dark and the leaping flames of a wood fire turn her trunk red. Some instinct warned her that danger was lurking, that it was close, very close. Every now and then, she would throw up her trunk and trumpet shrilly and all the other elephants would join in, till the ground rumbled with their thunder. The mahouts would curse and shout to their charges to be quiet. They spoke to them, rubbed their trunks, tickled behind their ears, offered them handfuls of grass. The camp would slowly re-settle down to sleep.

Again there was the jungle silence, broken by the splitting of a dry bamboo, or the shrill scream of a victim pounced on by an enemy. Under the trees wheeled and flitted small bats and larger bats, ghostly shadows which uttered shrill squeaks in so high a key as to be almost inaudible. There were moths, immense white or cream moths attracted by the light of fires and lanterns. There were beetles and flying ants in their thousands. Mosquitoes zinged in millions, and down by the river came the raucous croaking of frogs; some staccato and shrill; others bellowing deep and sonorous like the huge kettledrums over the entrance to a palace.

Only the elephants in their lines remained awake, swaying to allay their restlessness and disquiet, perhaps also to ease the enormous weight off their feet. They scented tiger.

Every night, Sher crouching low, crept round the camp to

74

spy out its weakness. He also felt nervous, but the bait of a calf was too alluring. Sometimes he came within feet of a hathi, who scenting him, would trumpet and squeal. His mahout would shout to be quiet. He would mutter: "Tis a baghi or a sher. Elephants always know.' He would look fearfully towards the jungle, now so dark and sinister, so full of ghosts and beasties which pounce in the night.

Once there came a flickering light wambling from the tents and a white man who gave orders. The mahouts scurried about vigilant and alert. Fruit and sugar was given to the Pearl. At first she refused them, her trunk swinging like a pendulum. Then it nosed to her mahout's hand, its queer mouth-tip open. She snatched the titbit and tossed it into her huge maw of a mouth. She went on rocking and swaying.

Sher watched and waited for three nights. Then, in the moonlight he saw that something was standing between the massive forelegs of the Pearl, something which every now and then she caressed with her trunk. Her calf had been born. Sher's eyes glistened.

He felt that he would only be able to cope with one elephant. So he crept close to the auntie. He could hear her rumble and snort and blow. He sensed her uneasiness. He sprang down in front of her and stood there, snarling in a low tone. She advanced a step, then another, feeling around with her trunk to seize her enemy. She could not see him for he was camouflaged in a shadow. Whenever the tip of her trunk came snaking near him, he struck at it savagely and bounded away. The terrible pain in the tenderest part of her body made the old lady squeal. Sher immediately attacked from the rear and sprang on to her hindquarters. She whirled about. Again and again Sher attacked, striking at her ears and lips, not seeking to kill, but to cause her pain. Thinking that she had to do with several tigers, old Rani screamed and panicked which was what he had intended she should do. She broke her hobble, rushed off into the jungle and crashed blindly about, trying to brush off the devil which clung to her ear.

Sher jumped clear and returned to attack the young mother. She stood with the calf safe under her. She was a terrifying sight with her trunk raised and her mouth open. Try as he could to reach the calf, there was always a leg or her trunk barring the way. She would lift a leg and try and crush him beneath it, or endeavour to curl her trunk round him.

The din was terrific, for by now all the other elephants were aroused. They trumpeted in chorus. From everywhere, men came running. Some carried lanterns; others flaming smoky torches. ''Tis a sher!' was the cry on everyone's lips.

The Pearl didn't help matters. In her concern for her baby, all the world had become her enemy. She even rounded on her own mahout when he tried to calm her. Temporarily insane with mother-love, she caught up the unfortunate man in her trunk, lifted him screaming in the air and dashed him to the ground. Then she knelt on him. Thus had her forbears acted in the days of the great Moguls when they had been trained to execute prisoners. It was feared that she would harm the calf who ran about squealing under her, his shrill baby trumpeting barely audible above her furious screams.

There was a brief consultation with the head mahout. 'Bring Bahadur and Jehangir.' One couldn't take risks when an elephant went mad. The Pearl was in an uncontrollable frenzy. It was death to come near her, and at any moment the other elephants might break loose, for they are animals who easily panic. Bahadur and Jehangir were old reliable beasts who instinctively knew what their mahouts wanted them to do without the latter using their heels or even a goad. When a youngster was

fractious, one of them would butt him in the ribs till he became obedient.

Within minutes the two monsters loomed up in the flare of the torches, silent and ghostly. Slowly, sedately, they rolled forward, wheeled and took up their places one on either side of the Pearl, pressing in against her flanks. At a word of command, they twined their trunks round hers, keeping them high out of harm's way, whilst men ran in to throw the great, iron-spiked anklets on to her legs. A huge ball of opium was cleverly tossed into her open mouth.

Slowly she calmed down. She ceased her trumpeting and allowed her wounds to be seen to, for now she was drowsy and perhaps realized that her precious baby was safe and sound.

Men were despatched to round up Rani who could be heard crashing and bellowing a mile away in the jungle. Several mahouts stayed near the Pearl in case she again became frightened. Everyone else reassured their charges that the danger was over.

Long before peace and quiet had been restored to the camp, Sher had slipped away before any of the mahouts had seen him. He felt frustrated and savage for having missed such a good dinner. Some of his ribs were very sore where a trunk had whacked across them.

Chapter *10*

THE TIGER HUNT

SHER AND a sherni were asleep in a patch of soft grass. Near the latter snuggled two very young cubs for Sher had found another mate and had become a proud father. They lay there relaxed at peace. Occasionally an ear or tail twitched when a fly alighted on them. Or paws galloped when the sleeper dreamt of hunting.

Sher woke up. He raised his head, blinked, and sprang to his feet, his tail twitching uneasily, apprehensively. Carried on the still air came the distant sounds of hammering and of men's voices.

Silently circling, Sher went through the jungle till he came to a glade where men were busy chopping down trees and tying branches on to another one to make a shooting platform. It was where two tracks met which Sher often used. A stranger shouted and yelled orders. Sher didn't like his smell, and he carried a gun, so he might be dangerous. A little apart the old hunter Budu squatted on his hunkers watching, his old eyes keen and alert.

Sher also watched, intently crouched under some bushes, unseen, unsuspected.

He saw the stranger helped up into the tree. His gun was handed to him and Budu climbed up by his side. A bleating, protesting goat was dragged along and tied up near the tree. The villagers left.

Everything became very quiet. Sher was curious and still very suspicious. Cautiously keeping to the shadows, he circled silently noting where the sportsman sat and what he could see. Why had a goat been tied up in the jungle at night? He suspected a trap. As silently as he had come he raced off to where he had left his family.

For a while the two older tigers stood listening, their ears cocked, their whiskers quivering. The cubs, not understanding what was the matter, started a rough and tumble game, rolling over and biting and clawing without doing each other any harm. Sher growled softly, a warning growl. The sherni understood. She turned and went off down a track leading to the low-lying ground by the river. The cubs ceased their play and padded off after her.

Sher snarled and returned grinning to the tree where the men were sitting. He wanted to find out more. A goat would be a pleasant change to deer. He had a sense of humour and he felt very cross. He would show them who was Lord of the Jungle.

When he was about a mile away, he sent out a shattering roar

F

which was answered by all the alarm cries of the jungle, by the belling of a sambhur, the harsh khok-khok of a langur and the shrill chatter of the small red monkeys.

In the tree Budu murmured. 'The tiger is a long way off. When he comes it will be without noise.'

Night fell and there was a great silence broken only by the buzz of mosquitoes and the troat-croak of bull-frogs. A broad leaf fluttered down and something which was not a leaf, but a bat, flitter-fluttered between the trees.

Again Sher roared his defiance and the jungle answered. Budu whispered. 'He comes this way. Watch the goat. He will know when the tiger comes.'

There came a third roar but no sight of the tiger. The goat bleated shrilly and was suddenly silent. Again silence. Then from every direction came angry arrghs. There was a burst of flame and a sharp explosion as the sportsman fired.

'He has killed the goat,' said Budu. 'He will not return tonight.'

Sher was extremely annoyed that someone should dare to come and disturb his jungle. He would teach him a lesson. Silently he slipped back in an opposite direction. He began to sharpen his claws on the tree-trunk. Screagh. Scre-eagh. He rubbed a flank against it and purred. He had another go of claw-sharpening and then lay down out of gun-sight directly under the shooting platform. It was full moon and the moonlight was almost as bright as day. A troop of monkeys went whooping across the glade. One of them spotted Sher. The whoops became agitated shrieks. Sher yawned and uttered another shattering 'Arrrgh!' He could smell the terror of the men above him.

Snarling he sprang at the tree; a huge paw showed for a second over the edge of the platform. Again he roared and went off, deliberately crashing through the bushes. He was bored with Man.

82

All the jungle was upset with the happenings of the night. No-one in it felt safe. The next day, they became aware that the jungle was being beaten and that its lord was being hunted from the back of an elephant. In the trees converging towards the more open grassland was a long crescent of beaters with sticks and tins. They shouted and yelled and banged, driving all before them. Some fifty yards behind them came another line. Any animal who had doubled back through the first line of beaters would again find his escape cut off.

A couple of deer came leaping by, anxiety in their eyes, their legs trembling. They were so close to the sherni that their flanks brushed against her; yet their terror was so great that they were quite unaware of her presence and she was far more concerned with her cubs' safety to think of striking, though she hadn't fed.

A young boar cantered past. Some partridges whirred up to settle again a little further on. More birds came flying and fluttering. They alighted only to rise again in alarm. A python, disturbed by the clamour, zigzagged between the grassy hummocks to seek refuge in a far-away hole.

From the back of an elephant it was easy to see over the top of the long grass which was higher than a man. All the movements of a driven creature could be followed by the ripples it made passing through the grass.

Worried by the sounds of the approaching shouts and yells and the beating of the drums and tins, the sherni bounded to her feet growling, her tail lashing angrily, her ears flat back on the top of her head. The cubs ceased their playing. Their baby eyes grew huge and round. They sensed that she was worried and came to her whimpering with fear. Snarling, she paced up and down uncertain what to do next.

The beaters came closer and closer. Their angry voices spread terror and the clash of metal even more so. She could hear the branches snapping and the swish of staves against bush and dry grass. The scent of Man was very strong. She could smell his nearness and glimpsed a raised arm.

She nosed the cubs into a thick clump of grass, hoping that its sharp saw-like edges would protect them. To create a diversion, she moved away and crouched, ready for action, her eyes blazed, every nerve and muscle was a-twitch.

Nearer and nearer came the beaters. There was a faint rustle in the grass close to her and a huge grey shape loomed up. It was that of an elephant.

Bahadur was an old, reliable beast, but he hated being taken by surprise. His mahout, seated behind the huge ears, coaxed him along. He promised him a reward of sugar and whispered that he was the bravest of elephants. Protesting and rumbling, Bahadur

84

cautiously rolled forward, his trunk held high out of the way of the sharp pampas grass.

'On my lord!' bellowed the mahout above the din of the yelling beaters. 'Careful, o Ruby of Excellence!'

As Bahadur stepped into the open space where the sherni was crouching, she sprang at him with a roar, clawing at the base of his trunk and underlip. Squealing with surprise and pain, he backed violently; then, with the sherni firmly hooked on to his face and shoulder and one of her paws fixed in the tender edge of an ear, he plunged about screaming and trumpeting. He tried to twine his trunk round the fiend to drag her loose. She ripped a deep cut down it. He tried to kneel and trample her under his huge feet. The mahout, thrown this way and that retained his seat only by a sheer miracle. The sportsman dropped his gun and clung on to the ropes of the padded shooting pad. No yelling of

85

orders, no use of the goad had the slightest effect. If anything they added to the elephant's terror. Bahadur plunged and ploughed like a ship in a heavy sea. Nothing that he did would dislodge the devil clinging to him.

Sherni screamed and roared. She realized her danger, that if she lost her grip and fell, she would be trampled to death. One of the jerks made her weight tear away the flesh she was hooked into and she slipped; but she managed to dig her claws into a cheek. It was all she could do to hold on.

Sher had been making his way back to rejoin the sherni when the beat started. The terrific din and the shouting terrified him. Why had all these noisy men come into his jungle? He bounded along a track and then stopped to listen, one paw raised. His head jerked nervously this way, that way. He sensed danger.

He padded on a few yards, came back, growled and swished his tail. He bounded high as a bamboo crashed against a tree. A frightened deer leapt past, a bird flew out of the thicket screeching, and he saw the head and shoulders of a yelling beater above the bushes. Snarling, he beat a hurried retreat to a tangle of thorn in which he crouched low, motionless and invisible.

After a few minutes he crept out and moved cautiously like a tawny ghost in the yellow sunshine. But always there was a screaming man barring his way. He had never been so frightened.

Then he heard the sherni's shrieks. His fury overcame his terror. He charged at a group of beaters, bounded over them and landed in front of Bahadur, a snarling, spitting avenger.

Two tigers were too much for the wounded elephant, who turned and bolted for the trees. The sudden diversion saved the sherni who slipped to the ground and streaked off through the long grass, over a stream to the safety of a deep ravine. Sher followed. For a moment he was seen as he leapt the water.

'They have gone to the Bara Nalah,' said Budu. 'It is a very dangerous place, too difficult to beat.'

So the hunt was called off and the beaters paid.

The two tigers crouched listening in a hollow under a rock. The sherni shivered and miawled. She was very shaken and anxious about her babies. Sher still rumbled angrily. He was so furious that once he struck out at her. She flattened herself back against the rock spitting.

After a couple of hours the jungle began to return to normal. Birds flew about. Noses poked out of the bushes; they sniffed and snuffed and their owners ventured forth. Sher crept out with the sherni nervously slinking behind.

They hunted up and down calling to the cubs. The whole place reeked of elephant and Man. The scent was very strong where the beaters had sat down to smoke and gossip. Miaow! Miaow! wailed the sherni. Aow! Aow! came back the faint echoes.

Suddenly a small paw shot out of the grass and caught hold of her tail-tip. There they were, her precious babies, quite safe and sound, for they had been good, obedient little cubs and hadn't moved from where she had left them. She nosed them and licked them all over whilst they danced round her trying to grab her whiskers.

Sher lay down on the path and pretended to take no notice of all the ridiculous fuss. Becoming bored, he yawned, got up and walked slowly down the path leading to the cave. The sherni watched him and went on licking behind a cub's ear. He growl-called. So she followed with the cubs tagging behind. The poor wee mites, not much bigger than a cat, lurched unsteadily after her; their fat little bodies were far too heavy for their baby legs.

One of them sat down, lifted up his nose and began to howl.

His mother came back, nosed him to make him stand up, but he rolled over on his back. Seeing how tired he was, she picked him up by the scruff of his neck and carried him. Immediately the other cub seeing that he was being left behind began to mew piteously.

Sher turned his head to see what the fuss was about. He watched her carry one cub a short distance and then return for the other, repeating this till the cave was reached. Uttering a low arrgh he went off to hunt.

Again both cubs were well licked all over, but they were far too tired and sleepy to mind being washed. Soon they were lying in a soft cuddly tangle. The tigress purred as she watched them, her eyes half closed; she was happy, at peace with all the world.

Suddenly she was up on her feet in front of them, growling, her ears back, her eyes flashing, ready to spring. But it was only Sher dragging a deer which he had just killed.

An hour later, all the family were peacefully asleep. The beat, the elephant, the screaming men were already half forgotten. To-morrow would be another day of sunshine and warmth and hunting.

The cubs grew up. When they were old enough they left their parents to go off into the jungle and find adventure for themselves. The sherni was unlucky, for she was caught in a trap and sent to the Zoo where people go to look at her. But she isn't unhappy for she is well fed and perhaps has forgotten all about the jungle, where Sher reigns as its lord and master.

Chapter *11*

AN EVENING STROLL

THE LORD of the Jungle, now a lonely old tiger, often went to a
secret glen. At one end of it the stream came down, deep and
rushing and narrow between tall black cliffs in which pigeons,
in their thousands, had their nests. A tree rooted in a crevice
hung outwards a-drip with great clusters of violet blossom and
masses of bright orange flowers fell in drifts from the ledges.

At a sudden noise the cliffs would become alive with thousands
of pigeons whirring out in a blue-grey and white flutter. They
would circle round a few times and then return home.

The stream cascaded over some rocks and then widened out into a series of wide shallow pools, with here and there a sandy beach or an outcrop of rock.

Sher liked to come to the glen and lie up unseen and concealed, whilst he watched what went on below him.

A nilghai came down to drink, a big blue-black bull with gentle eyes and small ugly horns and square-cut body. Every now and then he blew through his nostrils making the water froth and bubble. Having drunk his fill the nilghai moved off, his gait jerky and angular.

A pair of hares slipped out of the long grass. One watched whilst the other drank. Their long legs and ears were apprehensive and tremulous, for Khargosh is a timorous beastie. His safety lies in his swift, jinking flight. The pair scented that Baghi had been recently down to drink and knew that panthers like to curl up on flat boulders from which they can spring down on to their prey. Baghi was a horrible enemy whose evil, green eyes mesmerized his unfortunate prey into standing still. The khargosh didn't linger. They went off bounding, their long thin legs moving by awkward jerks.

A pair of otters came frisking out of their holt, a hole in an overhanging bank, followed by four young cubs. They were a charming sight as they played and rolled and tumbled, now in the water, now on the sand. Their sire leapt up on to a high rock and stared into the deep pool below it, his eyes alert, his whiskers quivering. Silently, swiftly, without making a splash, his lithe body slid into the water. A minute later he surfaced with a fair-sized mahseer in his mouth, plump and silvery and glittering in the sun. The cubs made a rush at it tearing the flesh off with their sharp teeth. Soon all that was left was a neatly cleaned backbone and tail. The cubs then had a grand time on the sand rolling about and nipping each other.

Something alarmed the older otters who sat up to peer around hissing and ck-ck-cking, all the bristles down their backs sticking up. The next moment all six of them were in the water swimming one behind the other to safety.

On the other side of a great boulder on the beach, Mor had been displaying his beautiful tail to his admiring hens. Suddenly he folded it up like one snaps a fan shut, rose in the air to fly to the further bank with his tail trailing out behind him. His wives, heads stretched out, scuttled low for some bushes.

Wondering what had alarmed both the otters and Mor, Sher raised his head, his eyes keenly alert for danger.

Shivering, he watched a python's blunt nose followed by many feet of beautiful mottled white-green and bronze body slide out of the tall grass and sinuously make its way over and between the rocks. Its head was slightly raised. Its tongue flick-flickered as it glided, avoiding anything sharp and prickly. Smooth as silk, the glossy glistening coils moved, swelling and elongating in a graceful ripple. In Sher's eyes, they were yards of indescribable evil. The snake lowered its head and lapped daintily, glancing about with its malevolent, mesmeric, lidless eyes. Having slaked its thirst, it nosed around for a smooth flat boulder in the sun. It selected one, a matching yellowish green in colour. The immense reptilian body slowly heaved itself upon it and coiled down with its head in the centre. It appeared to be but one boulder on the top of another. Only when another animal came near, did the evil head raise itself an inch and the tongue start its unceasing flicker.

It was very peaceful in the glen for Man seldom went there. Many birds came down to drink and left their tracks on the sandy patches. These were criss-crossed by the claws of plover and partridge, of peacock, jungle fowl, and finch. Some hopped, some ran, others stalked or strutted. They called and peeped and

92

whistled to each other; squabbled and quarrelled noisily, pecked and clawed.

A hoopoe came down to peck amongst the stones. She alighted spreading out her black and white barred skirts and her golden crest slowly subsided on her head. She strutted about, poking her immensely long curved beak into every cranny. She pecked several times sharply at something which wriggled and then flew away. It was a large, reddish-brown scorpion. Another, disturbed by the bird, scuttled out from under a stone. Immediately, their tails curved up in the air over their bodies, the pair circled each other crabwise. Every now and then one of them struck with the venomous point. Then they disappeared down a crack.

A water wagtail with his long tail lifting and dipping, scurried about busy pecking here, pecking there. He gave the impression of swimming on land. He was a happy, elegant little bird, much

93

liked by the villagers for whom his arrival meant also that of the winter.

A flight of parrots went over screeching and changed their direction sharply when they saw Sher. They flew so low that he could see the brilliant red band round their necks against the bright-green plumage.

Shifting his position to ease cramp, he turned his head and saw a flash of gold between the trees followed by another as a pair of golden orioles wheeled and weaved in and out.

Fish rose plop-plopping where the river ran wide and shallow. Near a clump of pink oleanders green-blue and scarlet-brown dragonflies skimmed above the surface of the water and darted in and out of the stems; the sun shone on and through their transparent gauze wings. They were so light, so swift that they could only be glimpsed for a second when they hovered. The water was so clear that from above every pebble and aquatic plant could be seen. Between them lay the fish, their bodies slowly moving to the current.

Now and then the pool rippled when a water beetle sped across. It made the reflections of the towering white plumes of siraki on the far bank blur and dance. Where there were reeds, frogs hopped and jumped. These reeds were a hunting-ground for a pair of sarus cranes. For hours on end, the tall grey birds with their scarlet caps would stand in the water waiting, watching. Suddenly a long spear of a beak would flash down and bring up a titbit, a struggling frog or a wriggling fish. The crane would throw it up in the air and neatly catch it head first and a bulge would slowly work down his long neck. Once more the crane would stand, his head hunched between his shoulders waiting, watching, Sometimes one would call mournfully. 'Sa-rus! Sa-rus!' to the other and the answer would come echoing back. These cranes mate for life and are always to be found in pairs, for

94

if anything happens to one of them, the other just pines away. When they became tired of fishing, they both took flight to another pool, as graceful in the air as they had been angular on the ground.

A rat came out of its hole by a twisted root. It ran out into the open after slight hesitation and found something to eat. It sat up holding the berry between its forepaws and nibbled rapidly at it, its bright eyes alert to everything around.

Suddenly there was a shrill whining screech like a falling bomb, and out of the blue sky, a hawk plummeted down, its wings close to its body. At the last possible moment, it braked with spread tail and rose with the rat dangling from its talons. It flew off to a tree to peck at its prey which it held down with its immensely powerful hooked claws. It held its head a bit on one side, continually on the look-out. Its eyes were fierce, merciless, and savage.

A troop of monkeys came screaming and whooping. Some remained in the trees whilst the others raced down to the water where they played tag or searched for beetles and snails. A couple of females sat together nodding and grunting like two old gossips. One of them industriously searched through every hair of her friend's neck. Their children, two skinny little beasts, scampered and gambolled near them, longing like little boys to go and explore. When one of them tried to do this, his mother grabbed him by the tail and soundly cuffed him. Two of the young males had a squabble. They bounced up and down on all fours screaming at each other, their lips snarling back from their yellow teeth. Then they stalked away slowly in opposite directions to express their indignant, hurt feelings.

Suddenly a sentinel on the tree khok-khokked. He had spotted the python who is Bandar's greatest enemy, for the latter likes to coil himself round a branch pretending to be part of it and so catches any unsuspecting monkey who comes bounding on to it. Immediately the alarm was taken up and the whole troop cantered out of sight.

The sun sank lower in the sky bathing everything in a translucent glow. The far hills changed their dusty greens and browns to delicate blue, mauve, citron, and vivid pink. The violet shadows lengthened and lay longer on the ground. The first flights of flying foxes came flitting across the evening sky on their way to their feeding-grounds. They flew slowly with tremendous sweeps of their wings. The birds twittered and squabbled and squawked as they settled down for the night, and the bats came out to flitter up and down, snapping at the midges and gnats.

The sun vanished behind a spur. All the bright colours of the water and hills and sky quickly faded. It was suddenly night and quite dark, for there is never any twilight in India.

With a low growl Sher got up, stretched and strode off stiffly and slowly to where the kakar would be grazing. His great paws turned in as he padded silently and his enormous head swung from side to side as he walked. His lower jaw dropped open and his tongue lolled. If his muzzle was greying and his fine whiskers no longer stood out fiercely, his great golden eyes missed nothing.

The Lord of the Jungle was taking his evening stroll.

Printed in Great Britain by Richard Clay & Company Limited Bungay · Suffolk